Little Burro

JIM ARNOSKY

G. P. PUTNAM'S SONS
An Imprint of Penguin Group (USA) Inc.

G. P. PUTNAM'S SONS
An imprint of Penguin Young Readers Group
Published by The Penguin Group
Penguin Group (USA) Inc., 375 Hudson Street, New York, NY 10014, USA

USA | Canada | UK | Ireland | Australia | New Zealand | India | South Africa | China
Penguin Books Ltd, Registered Offices: 80 Strand, London WC2R 0RL, England

For more information about the Penguin Group, visit penguin.com

Library of Congress Cataloging-in-Publication Data
Arnosky, Jim, author, illustrator. Little Burro / Jim Arnosky.
pages cm
Summary: "When Little Burro's band of burros leaves her canyon, Little Burro does not want
to follow, but she soon finds out that visiting new places can be fun"—Provided by publisher.
1. Donkeys—Juvenile fiction. [1. Donkeys—Fiction.] I. Title.
PZ10.3.A86923Lg 2013   [E]—dc23   2012048875

Published simultaneously in Canada.
Manufactured in China by South China Printing Co. Ltd.
ISBN 978-0-399-25519-9
Special Markets ISBN 978-0-399-25597-7 NOT FOR RESALE
1 3 5 7 9 10 8 6 4 2

Design by Ryan Thomann. Text set in Perrywood.
The art for this book was done in acrylic paint and white chalk.

ALWAYS LEARNING   PEARSON

This Imagination Library edition is published by Penguin Group (USA), a Pearson
company, exclusively for Dolly Parton's Imagination Library, a not-for-profit
program designed to inspire a love of reading and learning, sponsored in part by The
Dollywood Foundation. Penguin's trade editions of this work are available wherever
books are sold.

For Sienna

Little Burro was born in a canyon on a hillside, in a soft sandy spot beside a big round rock.

It was her favorite place.

The hillside was breezy and cool in the middle of the hot desert day . . .

. . . and warm and cozy at night, when the sun had gone away.

Little Burro was the only little burro in a band of wild burros.

They lived in the cozy canyon, eating dry twigs and water-filled cactus plants.

One morning, the burro band
began to leave their hillside home.

Little Burro hee-hawed loudly,
crying out to make them stay.

When they did not stay, she
turned her back and would not
watch them walk away.

Only when her mother began
walking, and called for her to come,
did Little Burro follow.

She followed her mother and the others along a narrow rocky trail.

The trail led the burros along a steep and slippery ledge.

The trail crossed hot desert sands.
With every burning step, Little Burro
was farther from her favorite place.

When they finally came to the end of the trail, the burro band began to run, racing toward a shimmering lake. It was their first visit since Little Burro had been born. Now she was big enough to make the trip.

Little Burro had never seen a lake before. It looked as big as the sky and just as blue.

Little Burro watched her mother
and the others drink from the lake.

She took a sip. The water was cool
and tasted good.

Some fish jumped. A frog swam by.

Little Burro jumped after the fish.

"Hee-haw!" she shouted excitedly.

She ran into the water, splashing the other burros.

"Hee-haw! Heee-haw!" they squealed to make Little Burro stop.

"Hee-haw!" she called back, splashing them again.

Little Burro played in the water all afternoon.

She was having so much fun, she did not want to leave.

Her mother and the others quenched their thirst and cooled their legs in the lake. When the sun began to go down, they headed back up the hill on the same trail they had come down.

Little Burro hee-hawed for them to come back to the water.

But the band of burros did not stop,
and Little Burro followed.

As they walked back on the steep trail,
the sun kept going down.

It was dark when they reached
the rocky hillside where Little Burro
was born.

   She found her favorite place beside
the big round rock and lay down for
the night. It was good to be home.

But she missed the shimmering lake where she drank and splashed in the cool water.

She missed the
fish jumping, and
the frog swimming.

She curled up tight and fell asleep and dreamed that she was splashing there again.

The lake was Little Burro's other favorite place.

AUTHOR'S NOTE

The wild burros that live in the American Southwest are descended from African and Asian burros that were brought here to carry supplies for early explorers, pioneers, and later miners of gold and silver.

While boating on a deep and crystal-clear Arizona lake, I saw my very first group of wild burros. I watched the small band walk single file all the way down a long, narrow, and steep canyon trail to the edge of the lake.

They grazed on green plants and wet their hooves in the cool water. Among them, one little burro stood close to its mother, eyeing our boat with what appeared to be a mixture of wariness and curiosity.

After a while, it lost interest in us and simply enjoyed the water with the others. The little burro was very young and small. I wondered if this was its first trip down the long, steep trail to the lake.

Years later, I remembered the wild burros and the canyon lake, and the story of Little Burro began to develop in my mind. First in words. Then in pictures.

The character of Little Burro captures much of the personality I saw in the little wild burro on the shore of that beautiful Arizona lake. I enjoyed writing and illustrating this story very much.

Jim Arnosky